THE SQUIGGLE

by Carole Lexa Schaefer

illustrated by Pierr Morgan

Dragonfly Books New York

My teacher
says, "Time
to walk to
the park."
So, as
always, off
we go in a
bunched-up,
slow,
tight,
straight
line.

I am last.
No one else sees what
I see on the sidewalk.

I grab it.

Slither slish.
It could be . . .

the dance of a big
scaly dragon.
Or . . .

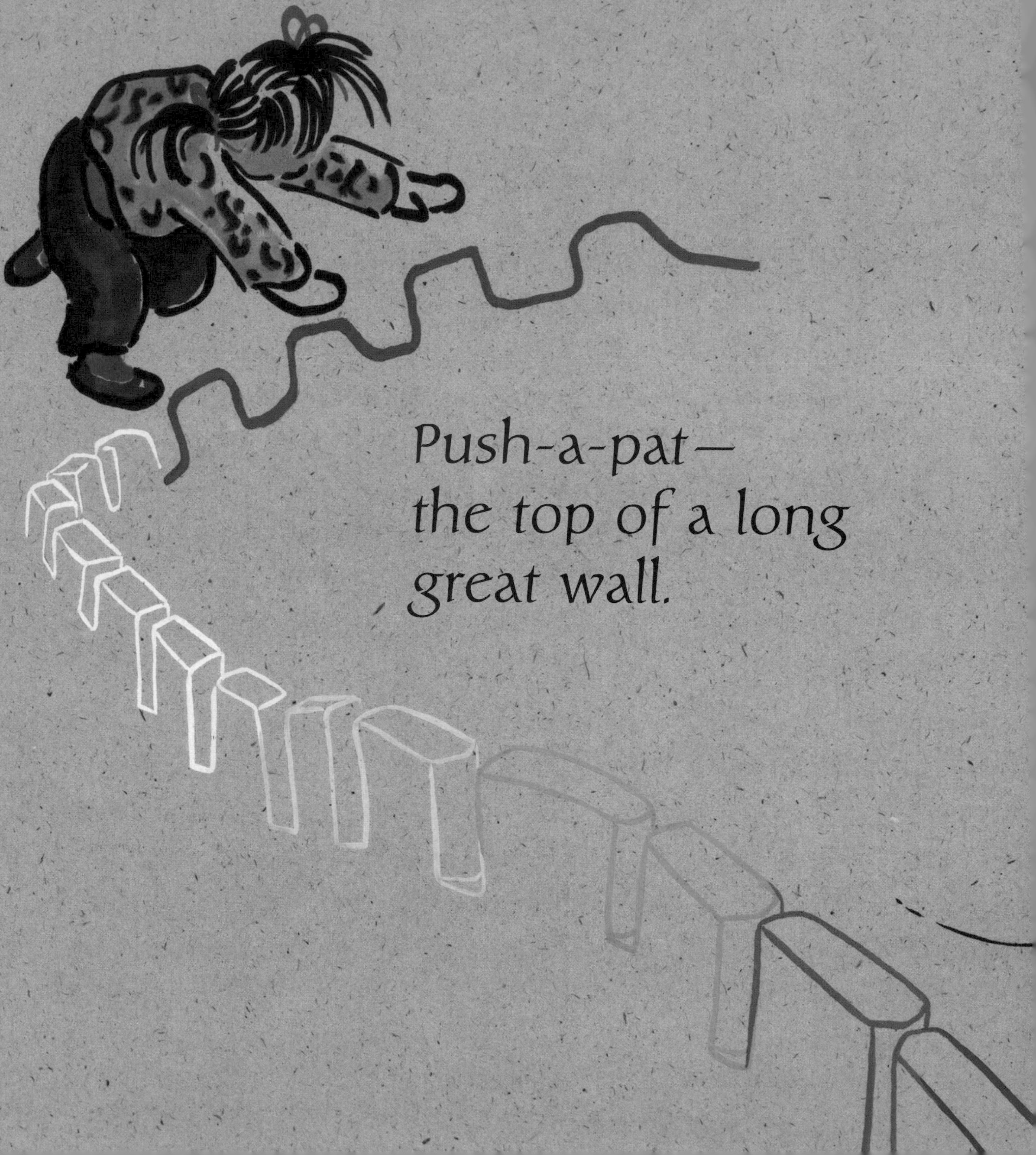

Push-a-pat—
the top of a long
great wall.

Snap, tah-dah.
Maybe it's the path
of a circus acrobat.
Or . . .

Crack crickle hiss—
the sky trail of
popping fireworks.

Tug KA-BOOM!
It might be the
poof of a stormy
thundercloud.
Or . . .

Ripple
shhh—
the circle of
a deep still
pool.
Or even . . .

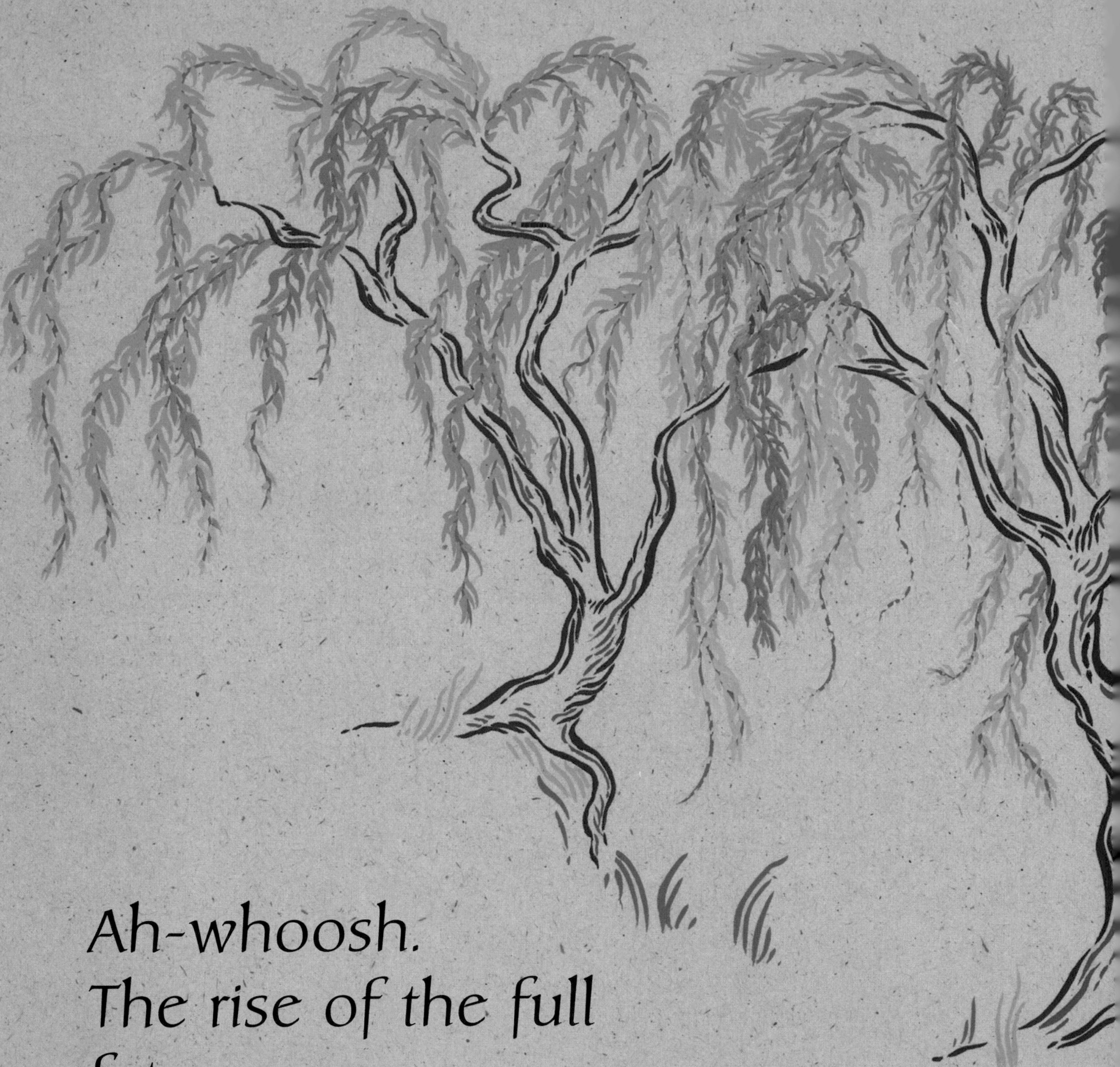

Ah-whoosh.
The rise of the full
fat moon.

Not so far ahead I see
my teacher and my class
shuffling along.
"Wait!" I call. "Look!"

Everyone turns around.

I show the dragon,

the wall,

the acrobat,

the fireworks,

the storm
cloud,

the pool,

and the moon.

Everyone is smiling.

"Hoorayee!"
they cheer,
and grab on, too.
Then, off we go
to the park in our
slither slish,
push-a-pat,
snap, tah-dah,
crack crickle hiss,
tug KA-BOOM!
ripple shhh,
ah-whoosh

squiggle of a line.

To Judy, Mary, and Dave, who inspired my childhood play.
And to Pierr, whose playful lines inspired this story.
—C.L.S.

To my teacher Agnes Haaga, a squiggler of all squigglers.
—P.M.

The art was done with Berol Prismacolor markers and
Winsor & Newton gouache on 80-lb., 100%-recycled
"Oatmeal" Speckle-tone paper from France.

 Published in the United States by Dragonfly Books, an imprint of Random House Children's Books, a division of Random House, Inc., New York. Originally published in hardcover in the United States by Crown Publishers, Inc., an imprint of Random House Children's Books, a division of Random House, Inc., New York, in 1996.

Dragonfly Books with the colophon is a registered trademark of Random House, Inc.

Visit us on the Web! www.randomhouse.com/kids

Educators and librarians, for a variety of teaching tools, visit us at
www.randomhouse.com/teachers

Library of Congress Cataloging-in-Publication Data
Schaefer, Carole Lexa.
The squiggle / by Carole Lexa Schaefer ; illustrated by Pierr Morgan.
p. cm.
Summary: As she walks to the park with her school class, a young girl finds a piece of string which her imagination turns into a dragon's tail, an acrobat, fireworks, a storm cloud, and more.
ISBN 978-0-517-70047-1 (hardcover) — ISBN 978-0-517-70048-8 (lib. bdg.) —
ISBN 978-0-517-88579-6 (pbk.)
[1. Imagination—Fiction. 2. String—Fiction.] I. Morgan, Pierr, ill. II. Title.
PZ7.S3315Sq 1996
[E]—dc20
95002299

MANUFACTURED IN CHINA

18 17 16 15 14 13 12 11 10

Random House Children's Books supports the First Amendment and celebrates the right to read.